Yannick Grotholt – Writer
Comicon – Artist

New York

LEGENDS OF CHIMA
#1 "High Risk!"

Yannick Grotholt – Writer
Comicon – Artist
Tom Orzechowski – Letterer
Max Gartman – Editorial Intern
Beth Scorzato – Production Coordinator
Michael Petranek – Editor
Jim Salicrup
Editor-in-Chief

ISBN: 978-1-62991-072-7 paperback edition
ISBN: 978-1-62991-073-4 hardcover edition

Printed in Canada
April 2014 by Friesens Printing
1 Printer Way
Altona, MB R0G 0B0

Papercutz books may be purchased for business or promotional use. For information on bulk purchases please contact Macmillan Corporate and Premium Sales Department at (800) 221-7945 x5442.

Distributed by Macmillan
First Papercutz Printing

HIGH RISK!
HA-HA! EAT MY DUST!
JUST YOU WAIT!
CHIMA-- A WORLD REIGNED OVER BY MIGHTY ANIMAL TRIBES, DIVIDED BY THE BATTLE OF THE NOBLE LIONS AGAINST THE EVIL SNEAKY CROCODILES. LAVAL, PRINCE OF THE LIONS, AND HIS FRIEND ERIS, A WARRIOR OF THE EAGLE TRIBE, ENGAGE IN A TRAINING RACE ON THEIR SPEEDORZ.

LOOK HOW QUICKLY THE TIDE TURNS!
I HAVE TO WIN, NO MATTER THE COST!
LOSING IS OUT OF THE QUESTION FOR THE LION PRINCE. SO HE TAKES DESPERATE MEASURES...
WHAT'S THE MATTER, ERIS--
--NEVER SEEN A LION FLY?
THE JUMP WENT WELL-- ALMOST. BUT A VINE SNAGGED LAVAL'S WHEEL.
UAAAAAAAAH

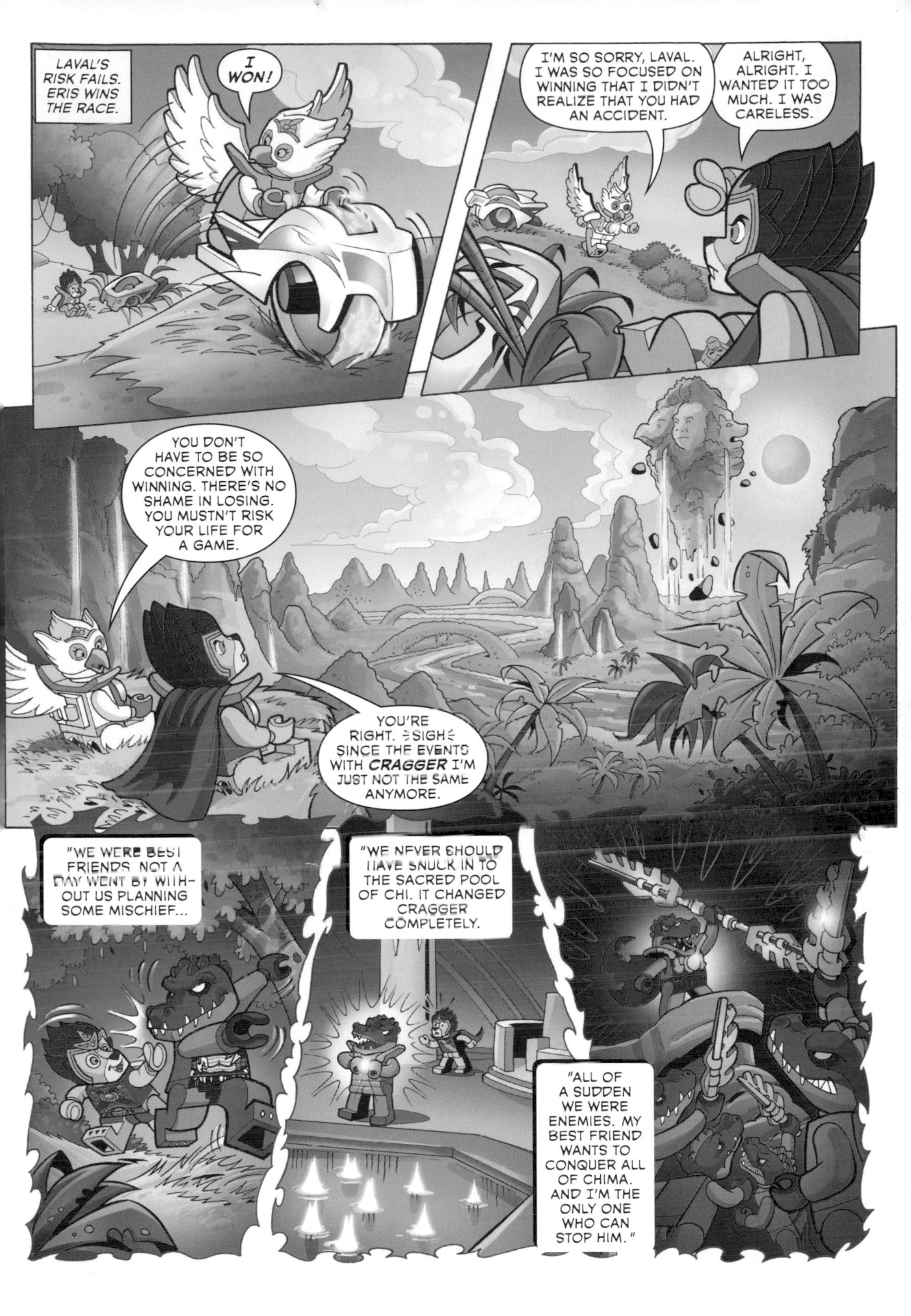
LAVAL'S RISK FAILS. ERIS WINS THE RACE.
I WON!
I'M SO SORRY, LAVAL. I WAS SO FOCUSED ON WINNING THAT I DIDN'T REALIZE THAT YOU HAD AN ACCIDENT.
ALRIGHT, ALRIGHT. I WANTED IT TOO MUCH. I WAS CARELESS.
YOU DON'T HAVE TO BE SO CONCERNED WITH WINNING. THERE'S NO SHAME IN LOSING. YOU MUSTN'T RISK YOUR LIFE FOR A GAME.
YOU'RE RIGHT. SIGH SINCE THE EVENTS WITH CRAGGER I'M JUST NOT THE SAME ANYMORE.
"WE WERE BEST FRIENDS. NOT A DAY WENT BY WITH-OUT US PLANNING SOME MISCHIEF...
"WE NEVER SHOULD HAVE SNUCK IN TO THE SACRED POOL OF CHI. IT CHANGED CRAGGER COMPLETELY.
"ALL OF A SUDDEN WE WERE ENEMIES. MY BEST FRIEND WANTS TO CONQUER ALL OF CHIMA. AND I'M THE ONLY ONE WHO CAN STOP HIM."

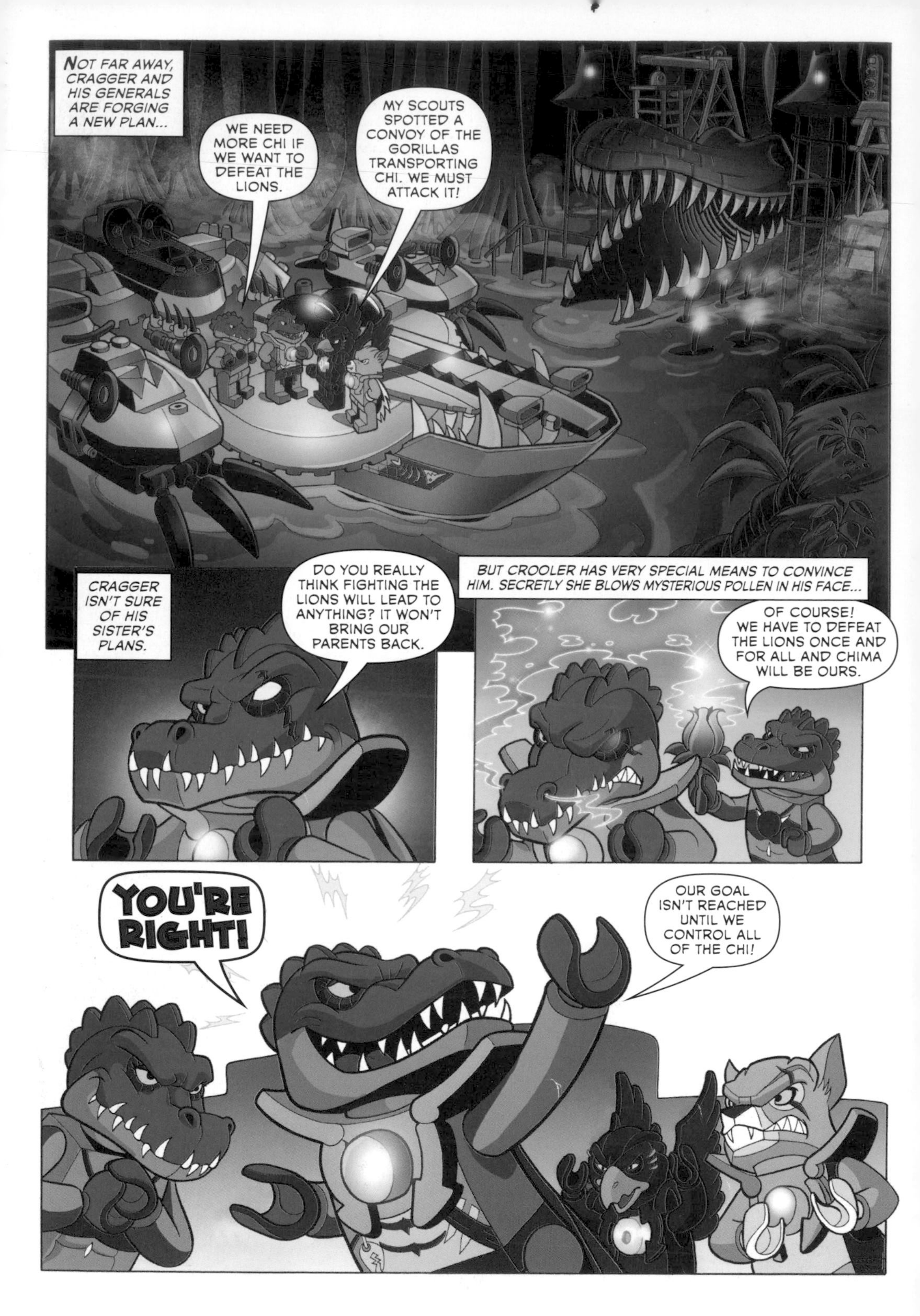
NOT FAR AWAY, CRAGGER AND HIS GENERALS ARE FORGING A NEW PLAN...
WE NEED MORE CHI IF WE WANT TO DEFEAT THE LIONS.
MY SCOUTS SPOTTED A CONVOY OF THE GORILLAS TRANSPORTING CHI. WE MUST ATTACK IT!
CRAGGER ISN'T SURE OF HIS SISTER'S PLANS.
DO YOU REALLY THINK FIGHTING THE LIONS WILL LEAD TO ANYTHING? IT WON'T BRING OUR PARENTS BACK.
BUT CROOLER HAS VERY SPECIAL MEANS TO CONVINCE HIM. SECRETLY SHE BLOWS MYSTERIOUS POLLEN IN HIS FACE...
OF COURSE! WE HAVE TO DEFEAT THE LIONS ONCE AND FOR ALL AND CHIMA WILL BE OURS.
YOU'RE RIGHT!
OUR GOAL ISN'T REACHED UNTIL WE CONTROL ALL OF THE CHI!

A SHORT TIME LATER, A CONVOY OF GORILLAS IS TRANSPORTING PRECIOUS CHI FROM THE TEMPLE OF THE LIONS TO THEIR HOME...
QUICK, QUICK, DUDES. WE HAVE TO GET THE CHI TO OUR BASE BEFORE IT GETS DARK.
AND BEFORE THE CROCODILE DUDES CAN SPOT US!

TOO LATE! RAZCAL ATTACKS WITH A CHI-RAIDER!
RRRAHARR! TAKE THIS, APES!
RETREAT! SAVE YOUR-SELVES!
RAZCAL CHASES THE GORILLAS DIRECTLY INTO A TRAP OF THE CROCODILES.
FINISH THEM AND GET THE CHI!

THE GORILLAS ARE LUCKY. LAVAL AND ERIS HAVE SPOTTED RAZCAL'S RAIDER ON THE HORIZON.
WE HAVE TO HELP THEM!
LAVAL! WE CAN'T GO IN THERE ALONE.
THE GORILLAS ARE TRYING TO FEND OFF THE CROCODILES AND THE WOLVES, BUT THEY DON'T STAND A CHANCE. THEY'RE SURROUNDED AND THEIR NUMBERS ARE FEW.
DON'T WORRY! I KNOW WHAT I'M DOING. BUT CALL FOR REINFORCE-MENTS!
I HOPE SOMEONE SEES THE FLARE...
FOOM
AS LAVAL ALMOST REACHES THE BATTLEFIELD...
NO TIME TO LOSE! THE GORILLAS CAN'T HOLD OUT MUCH LONGER.

HERE I COME!
YOU'RE NO MATCH FOR ME!
ARGH!
BUT MORE AND MORE ATTACKERS ARE SOON SURROUNDING LAVAL...
STAY AWAY!
...UNTIL HE HAS NO OTHER OPTION THAN TO SURRENDER.
HEY! TAKE IT EASY!
AND NOW GET THE CHI! LOAD IT INTO THE CHI RAIDER!

WELL, WELL. LOOKS LIKE WE NOT ONLY GOT OUR HANDS ON SOME PRECIOUS CHI, BUT ALSO A LION!
WELL, LAVAL. HOW DOES IT FEEL-- KNEELING BEFORE YOUR FUTURE KING?
WHAT HAS BECOME OF YOU, OLD FRIEND?
REINFORCEMENTS HAVE ARRIVED! CAN THEY TURN THE TIDE?
AAAAH!
KABOOM
YES! ANOTHER INTERCEPTOR IS TAKING DOWN A CHI RAIDER WITH A WELL-AIMED ROCKET.
AND HELP BY LAND ARRIVES!
TAKE THAT, UGLY REPTILES!

CRAGGER IS BACK ON HIS FEET AND USES THE DISTRACTION TO GRASP THE MOMENT...
GET A BAG WITH CHI, RAZCAL! AND THEN, LET'S GO!
AT LEAST WE'LL BE ABLE TO SECURE THESE TWO BAGS OF CHI.
THOSE MEAN COWARDS. THEY'RE NOT GETTING AWAY FROM ME!

CRAGGER... WE'VE GOT A PROBLEM!
NOTHING THAT WE CAN'T SHAKE OFF. GO!
VROOOM

SHAKING OFF LAVAL ISN'T AS EASY AS EXPECTED. LAVAL SLOWLY CATCHES UP AND DRAWS HIS SWORD...
CRASH
YOU MAY HAVE GOTTEN THE RAVEN. BUT YOU WON'T GET ME.
THEN LAVAL DISCOVERS AN OVERTURNED TRUNK...
HMMM...
OH, NO... LAVAL ISN'T GOING TO...

HE IS! BUT THIS TIME HE THOUGHT THINGS THROUGH...
WOOOHOOO!
DON'T LEAVE SO SOON, CRAGGER!
HUH? WHERE IS HE?
ALL GOOD THINGS COME FROM ABOVE!
HUAARGH!
PRACTICE MAKES PERFECT.
--WELL, ALMOST!

YOU DARE CROSS MY PLANS?
HUP!
GET OFF OF ME!

TAKE YOUR CLAWS OFF MY SON!
UH, OH...
I'LL BE BACK... THAT'S FOR SURE!
HOP

I'M SO HAPPY THAT YOU'RE ALRIGHT. LUCKILY YOU THOUGHT TWICE THIS TIME BEFORE RISKING YOUR NECK.
I'M PROUD OF YOU, SON. NOT ONLY DO YOU HAVE THE SPEED OF A LION, BUT ALSO THE WITS!
I'M NOT SURE ABOUT THAT, FATHER. I WON'T BE SATISFIED UNTIL I CAN CONVINCE CRAGGER THAT HE'S WRONG AND END THIS SENSELESS BATTLE.
THE END

A SPARK OF Friendship
THE EAGLES HAVE ISSUED AN INVITATION TO A MAJOR SPEEDORZ TOURNAMENT. KING LAGRAVIS HAS DECIDED TO ARRIVE A DAY EARLY. THERE ARE STILL A FEW VERY IMPORTANT ISSUES HE WISHES TO DISCUSS WITH HIS ALLIES...
IN THE MEANTIME, LAVAL TAKES A DETOUR THROUGH THE FALLING JUNGLE. HE IS DETERMINED TO TEST HIS SPEEDOR SKILLS BEFORE THE TOURNAMENT BEGINS...
THIS SHORT CUT MAY BE A LITTLE RISKY...

BUT LIFE IS TOO SHORT NOT TO TAKE RISKS!
AND, LIFT-OFF!

LAVAL HAS RARELY FELT BETTER PREPARED THAN HE DOES TODAY...
WITH MY FLYING SKILLS THE TOURNAMENT TOMORROW WILL BE CHILD'S PLAY!

A FEW HOURS LATER, LAVAL HAS REACHED THE EAGLES' CASTLE...
I DON'T BELIEVE IT!
HIS FATHER HAS ALSO ARRIVED.
HOW DID THEY GET HERE BEFORE ME?
EWALD, THE LEADER OF THE EAGLES' RULING COUNCIL, WELCOMES THE LIONS. LAVAL IS APPALLED WHEN HE LEARNS WHO ELSE IS TAKING PART IN THE TOURNAMENT...
LAGRAVIS. IT IS GOOD THAT YOU WERE ABLE TO COME EARLIER. WE CAN TALK IN PEACE WITHOUT THE CROCODILES EAVESDROPPING ON US.
WHAT? THE CROCODILES ARE COMING TOO?!
THEY WOULD ONLY CAUSE US MORE TROUBLE IF WE HADN'T INVITED THEM.
BUT OUR LAST TOURNAMENT HAD TO BE ABANDONED BECAUSE CRAGGER ATTACKED ERIS! BELIEVE ME, YOU DON'T WANT HIM AROUND!
LAVAL, PLEASE ACCEPT EWALD'S DECISION. IT IS THE EAGLES WHO ARE ORGANIZING THE TOURNAMENT. NOT US.

MEANWHILE, CRAGGER AND CROOLER ARE ALREADY HATCHING THEIR NEXT SNEAKY PLOT IN THE CROC SWAMP HIDEOUT...
CRUG! CRAWLEY! WHEN WILL YOU FINALLY HAVE MY SPEEDOR READY? I WANT TO PROVE TO LAVAL THAT I'M THE BETTER DRIVER.
LITTLE BROTHER, HAVE YOU HAD TIME TO THINK ABOUT MY BRILLIANT PLAN?

PLAN? AH, THE PLAN! TO BE HONEST, I DON'T REALLY KNOW WHAT TO THINK. I DON'T WANT LAVAL TO BE--
THAT'S A PITY. BUT PERHAPS I CAN STILL MANAGE TO PERSUADE YOU.
ONCE AGAIN, CROOLER BEFUDDLES HER TWIN BROTHER'S SENSES WITH A MYSTERIOUS PLANT...
FROM ONE MOMENT TO THE NEXT, CRAGGER IS LIKE A DIFFERENT PERSON!
LET'S TEACH LAVAL A LESSON HE WON'T SOON FORGET.
THAT'S EXACTLY WHAT I WANTED TO HEAR.
LET'S SHOW THE LIONS!

THE BIG SPEEDORZ TOURNAMENT BEGINS THE NEXT MORNING. INHABITANTS FROM ALL OVER CHIMA HAVE MADE THE LONG JOURNEY TO EAGLES' CASTLE. LIONS, WOLVES, RHINOS, RAVENS, GORILLAS, BEARS--AND UNFORTUNATELY, ALSO THE CROCODILES...
INHABITANTS OF CHIMA! PLEASE ACCEPT OUR MOST CORDIAL WELCOME TO THIS YEAR'S EAGLE TOURNAMENT.
THE OBJECT OF THE CONTEST IS TO DRIVE OVER THE RAMP AND PUSH THE OPPONENT OFF HIS SPEEDOR WITH THE LANCE. THE FIRST COMBATANTS TO FACE EACH OTHER ARE WORRIZ THE WOLF AND GORZAN THE GORILLA.
BEGIN!
WHERE CAN CRAGGER HAVE GONE TO? SOMETHING'S NOT RIGHT HERE...
WORRIZ IS BRIEFLY DISTRACTED. ONE SHORT MOMENT OF INATTENTIVENESS IS ENOUGH TO LOSE THE ROUND.
A WELL DESERVED VICTORY FOR THE GORILLAS!
DUDE!

AND ERIS IS THE WINNER OF THE SECOND ROUND! I NOW ASK LAVAL AND CRAGGER TO TAKE UP THEIR STARTING POSITIONS.
I-- I HAVEN'T BEEN UP TO ANYTHING FISHY.
ON YOUR MARKS... GET SET... *GO!*
HOLD TIGHT, FUR BALL. THIS IS GOING TO BE THE RIDE OF YOUR LIFE!
DON'T WORRY. I'VE NEVER BEEN BETTER PREPARED.
LAVAL AND CRAGGER ARE RACING TOWARDS EACH OTHER...
WHAT--?!
...WHEN THEY ARE SUDDENLY TORN FROM THEIR SPEEDORZ BY TWO RAVEN'S CLAWS!

A MURMUR GOES THROUGH THE CROWD! THE CLAWS BELONG TO RAZCAL'S GLIDER!
WHY ARE THE RAVENS KIDNAPPING LAVAL AND CRAGGER?
DON'T THINK WE'RE GETTING ANY SHINY THINGS FOR THIS. WE'RE NOT.... REALLY WE AREN'T... OKAY, MAYBE WE ARE. BUT JUST A FEW.
EWALD, I DEMAND THAT YOU DO EVERYTHING IN YOUR POWER TO SAVE MY SON!
DO NOT WORRY, LAGRAVIS. EWAR WILL BRING BACK LAVAL AND PUNISH THE CULPRITS.
I WILL NOT DISAPPOINT YOU.
EWAR IMMEDIATELY JUMPS INTO HIS EAGLE INTERCEPTOR...
RAZCAL MAY HAVE A GOOD HEAD START. BUT EWALD IS ONE OF THE BEST PILOTS IN THE EAGLE TRIBE!
I HOPE YOU ARE RIGHT!

ABOVE THE CLOUDS, LAVAL AND CRAGGER ARE AT LOGGERHEADS AS USUAL!
THIS STUNT HAS GOT YOUR NAME WRITTEN ALL OVER IT, SWAMP-FACE. WHAT'S THE BIG IDEA?
I KIDNAP THE LION PRINCE AND DEMAND A FEW CHI ORBS FROM HIS TRIBE AS RANSOM. AN INGENIOUS PLAN!
EWAR IS SPARING NO EFFORT TO THWART CRAGGER'S PLAN. HE HAS ALMOST CAUGHT UP WITH THE GLIDER!
YOU DON'T KIDNAP YOUR BEST FRIEND.
BUT YOU DO KIDNAP YOUR FORMER BEST FRIEND.
HEY! STAY IN YOUR MACHINE, YOU PESKY FLY!
BY ORDER OF EWALD, THE GREAT EAGLE, YOU'RE UNDER ARREST!
NOBODY GETS TO TAKE US RAVENS. NO MATTER WHAT FOR.
RAZCAL ACCIDENTALLY HITS THE JOYSTICK OPERATING THE RAVEN'S CLAWS...

IS THIS ALSO PART OF YOUR BRILLIANT PLAN?
I'M NOT SURE. TO BE HONEST, THE IDEA FOR THE PLAN CAME FROM CROO--

-OOOOLER!

LUCKILY, LAVAL AND CRAGGER LAND ON SOFT SAND...
NORMALLY I HATE SAND. BUT NOT TODAY.

THIS IS ANOTHER FINE MESS YOU'VE GOTTEN US INTO!
THIS ISN'T NORMAL SAND... IT'S ***QUICK-SAND!***

IF WE HAD CHI NOW, WE COULD SAVE OUR-SELVES. BUT YOU LIONS ALWAYS HAVE TO BE SO MEAN WITH THE CHI ORBS!
LAVAL REMEMBERS HIS FATHER'S WORDS.
"NATURE IS NOT YOUR ENEMY, BUT YOUR FRIEND." THE BRANCH!
STEADY! I CAN ALMOST REACH IT!
MIND WHERE YOU PUT YOUR FEET, YOU OVERSIZED CAT!

TAKE MY HAND!
CRAGGER HESITATES. DOES HE REALLY WANT TO BE RESCUED BY A LION? BUT THE QUICKSAND IS THREATENING TO SLOWLY SWALLOW HIM.
YOU SEE, WE CAN SAVE OURSELVES WITHOUT CHI--
SPARE ME YOUR WORDS OF WISDOM. YOU SOUND WORSE THAN YOUR FATHER!

HOURS LATER, LAVAL AND CRAGGER STILL HAVEN'T FOUND THEIR WAY BACK HOME...
WE SHOULD HAVE TURNED LEFT AFTER THE HUMMING SUMMIT. BUT YOU WOULDN'T LISTEN TO ME!
TRUST ME. THE GORGE OF ETERNAL DEPTH SHOULD BE JUST AHEAD OF US.
YOU SAID THAT HOURS AGO. NOW I DECIDE WHICH WAY WE GO.
LAVAL?
THE YOUNG WARRIORS HAVE SET OFF A LANDSLIDE. LAVAL IS CLINGING WITH ALL HIS STRENGTH TO THE EDGE OF THE CHASM...
CRAGGER! HELP ME!

AT THIS MOMENT, CROOLER AND HER CROCODILE MINIONS APPEAR BY THE CHASM...
HERE YOU ARE! WE'VE BEEN SCOURING THE WHOLE OF CHIMA TRYING TO FIND YOU.
WHAT HAVE WE HERE? A DANGLING LION? PUT AN END TO IT, LITTLE BROTHER. THEN THE CHI IS OURS, ONCE AND FOR ALL!
CRAGGER... PLEASE... I CAN'T HOLD ON MUCH LONGER.
CRAGGER IS TORN THIS WAY AND THAT. SHOULD HE MAKE HIS SISTER AND HIS TRIBE PROUD OR SAVE LAVAL FROM FALLING?
FINALLY, HE GRASPS THE LION'S PAWS...
...AND DOES THE ONLY RIGHT THING-- HE RESCUES LAVAL.
THAT IS NOT WHAT WE AGREED.
I HAVE AN EVEN BETTER PLAN. JUST WAIT AND SEE.
THANK YOU, CRAGGER-- I THINK.

YOU ARE SURROUNDED. WE ARE TAKING YOU TO THE EAGLE'S CASTLE.
LET THEM GO, EWAR. WE ARE NOT LIKE THE CROCODILES.
AS YOU WISH. BUT I AM AFRAID YOUR FATHER WILL NOT BE PLEASED...
HE WILL UNDER-STAND.
DON'T GET ANY FUNNY IDEAS. I ONLY SAVED YOU BECAUSE YOU PULLED ME OUT OF THE QUICKSAND.
I MAY NOT UNDERSTAND, BUT I WILL OBEY.
AS CRAGGER AND HIS CROCODILE CREW DEPART...
DESPITE HIS WORDS, I SUSPECT CRAGGER ACTED NOT OUT OF ANY SENSE OF OBLIGATION--
--BUT OUT OF FRIENDSHIP! I HOPE I'M NOT MISTAKEN.
FAREWELL, OLD FRIEND!
THE END

CHIMA RESEMBLES A WASTELAND. THE DESPICABLE SCORPIONS, SPIDERS AND BATS HAVE DRAINED THE SACRED POOL OF CHI AND ARE HOLDING THE LEGEND BEASTS CAPTIVE. YET THERE IS STILL HOPE...
≡GRRR≡ I CAN'T STAND THE SIGHT OF THIS!
THE SPIDER TOURNAMENT
SLURP
SMACK

EACH TRIBE HAS SELECTED ITS MOST CAPABLE WARRIOR AND SENT HIM INTO THE TREACHEROUS OUTLANDS. IT IS NOW DOWN TO LAVAL, CRAGGER, ERIS, WORRIZ, GORZAN, ROGON, RAZAR, AND BLADVIC TO RESCUE THE LEGEND BEASTS FROM THE CLUTCHES OF THEIR ENEMIES AND TO SAVE CHIMA. SO FAR, THE EIGHT HEROES HAVE FOUND ONLY THE CROCODILE LEGEND BEAST.
FORTUNATELY, LAVAL AND THE OTHERS MUST NOT FACE THE PERILS OF THE OUTLANDS ALONE. LAVERTUS, THE ENIGMATIC HERMIT LION, SUPPLIES THE FRIENDS WITH WEAPONS, ARMOR AND... CUPCAKES?!
THERE YOU ARE, LAVAL.
YOU HAVE A TRULY LEGENDARY APPETITE.
SNAP

THE ATTACK OF THE SPIDERS AND BATS HAS ONE GOOD THING ABOUT IT. THE TRIBES OF CHIMA HAVE PUT ASIDE THEIR DIFFERENCES AND ARE ONCE MORE FIGHTING SIDE-BY-SIDE. EVEN LAVAL AND CRAGGER ARE THE BEST OF FRIENDS AGAIN!
DON'T FORGET YOUR ARMOR. YOU'LL NEED IT IN THE OUTLAND!
THANKS, CRAGGER.
YET LAVAL SEEMS SOMEWHAT LOW-SPIRITED TODAY. THE LION WARRIOR MISSES HIS KINGDOM.
FANCY A RACE THROUGH LAVERTUS'S DEFENSE OBSTACLE COURSE?
I'D RATHER TAKE PART IN A PROPER SPEEDORZ TOURNAMENT. HEY, WHAT'S THIS?
LOOKS LIKE AN INVITATION FROM KING LAGRAVIS.
THE LAST GRAND SPEEDORZ TOURNAMENT IN CHIMA IS TAKING PLACE TODAY.
WE COULD DRIVE TO THE LION TEMPLE AND TAKE PART IN THE RACE! WE COULD USE THE GOLDEN ORB FOR OUR QUEST!
OUT OF THE QUESTION. WE STILL HAVE TO FIND THE SEVEN LEGEND BEASTS. UP TO NOW WE HAVEN'T EVEN DISCOVERED A TRACE OF THEM. OUR TRIBES NEED CHI, TOO. WE MUST NOT NEGLECT THAT.
I'M GOING TO TAKE A LITTLE NAP. DON'T YOU DARE DISTURB ME.

IN THE MEANTIME, THE SPIDERS HAVE ALSO GOTTEN WIND OF THE TOURNAMENT...

WHAT IS IT, SPARRATUS? HAVE YOU FOUND A CURE FOR MY BOREDOM?
THAT I HAVE, MY QUEEN. THE INHABITANTS OF CHIMA ARE HOLDING THEIR LAST SPEEDORZ TOURNAMENT. THIS IS OUR CHANCE TO STEAL THEIR GOLDEN CHI.
THAT GIVES ME AN IDEA-- WE WILL SIMPLY HOLD OUR OWN SPEEDORZ TOURNAMENT!

BUT BEGGING YOUR PARDON, YOUR MAJESTY. WE SPIDERS DO NOT HAVE ANY SPEEDY-WHEELY-THINGIES!
THEN WE SHALL PROCURE SOME. SPARATTUS, GET US A FEW OF THOSE CHI-CONTROLLED NECK-BREAKERS.
VERY GOOD, MY QUEEN.
THE SPIDER QUEEN'S BOREDOM HAS QUICKLY VANISHED INTO THIN AIR...
THIS WILL BE FUN!

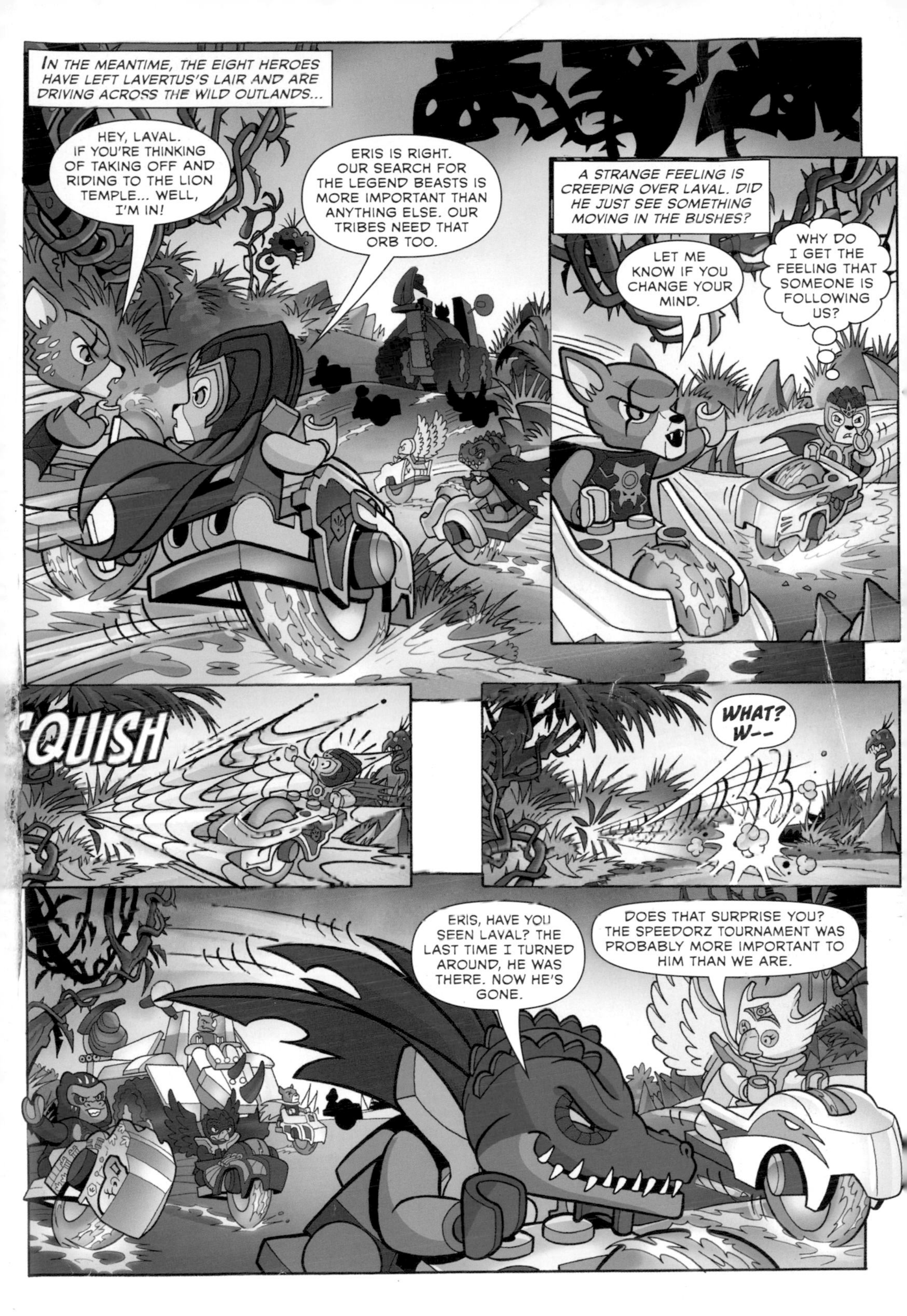
IN THE MEANTIME, THE EIGHT HEROES HAVE LEFT LAVERTUS'S LAIR AND ARE DRIVING ACROSS THE WILD OUTLANDS...
HEY, LAVAL. IF YOU'RE THINKING OF TAKING OFF AND RIDING TO THE LION TEMPLE... WELL, I'M IN!
ERIS IS RIGHT. OUR SEARCH FOR THE LEGEND BEASTS IS MORE IMPORTANT THAN ANYTHING ELSE. OUR TRIBES NEED THAT ORB TOO.
A STRANGE FEELING IS CREEPING OVER LAVAL. DID HE JUST SEE SOMETHING MOVING IN THE BUSHES?
LET ME KNOW IF YOU CHANGE YOUR MIND.
WHY DO I GET THE FEELING THAT SOMEONE IS FOLLOWING US?
SQUISH
WHAT? W--
ERIS, HAVE YOU SEEN LAVAL? THE LAST TIME I TURNED AROUND, HE WAS THERE. NOW HE'S GONE.
DOES THAT SURPRISE YOU? THE SPEEDORZ TOURNAMENT WAS PROBABLY MORE IMPORTANT TO HIM THAN WE ARE.

LAVAL SLOWLY COMES ROUND...
WHERE... WHERE AM I?
IN A CAVE IN SPIDER CANYON.
SHADOWIND!
WHAT ARE YOU DOING HERE?
THE SPIDERS AMBUSHED ME AND TOOK MY SPEEDOR. GUESS THEY DID THE SAME WITH YOU.
GRRRRR!
NNNG... PHEW
DON'T BOTHER TRYING. THE BARS ARE MADE OF INDESTRUCTIBLE SPIDER STEEL.
GET YOUR SKINNY SPIDER FINGERS OFF MY SPEEDOR!

SPARRATUS PAYS ABSOLUTELY NO ATTENTION TO LAVAL. HE STARTS THE SPEEDOR AND WHIZZES THROUGH THE CAVE. BUT HE DOESN'T EXACTLY CUT A GOOD FIGURE...
SWOOSH

AND THAT'S NOT EVEN HIS FIRST ATTEMPT.

EEEEKKK

ENOUGH! THE SIGHT OF YOU IS ENOUGH TO GIVE ME WRINKLES. IF I GET MY FIRST GREY HAIR BECAUSE OF YOU...
BUT THEN WHO IS TO RIDE THE SPEEDY-WHEELIES, YOUR MOST BEAUTIFUL HIGHNESS?
HMM. WHAT ABOUT THESE TWO PRISONERS HERE?

I WILL GRANT FREEDOM TO THE WINNER OF THE TOURNAMENT. THE LOSER SHALL MASSAGE MY LEGS FOR ALL ETERNITY. SO ACTUALLY, THERE ARE ONLY WINNERS!

YOUR FIRST TASK WILL BE TO REACH THE SUMMIT SAFELY. BUT BE WARNED: IF YOU TRY TO ESCAPE, MY SOLDIERS WILL SQUASH YOU LIKE FLIES.
NERVOUS, KID?
DREAM ON.
AND SO THE SPIDER TOURNAMENT BEGINS. LAVAL, WHO HAS OFTEN DODGED THE FALLING BRANCHES IN THE FALLING JUNGLE, PASSES THE TEST WITH FLYING COLORS...
KLONK
BUT SHADOWIND HAS TO CUT THE ROUND SHORT.
YES! I WON!
DON'T COUNT YOUR CHICKENS BEFORE THEY HATCH!

THE NEXT CHALLENGE IS TO CROSS THE RAVINE BETWEEN THE TWO MOUNTAINS OVER ROPE BRIDGES MADE OF COBWEBS.
THE LION WARRIOR LEADS 1 TO NOTHING. BUT DON'T WORRY. EACH OF YOU STILL HAS THE CHANCE TO BECOME MY PRIVATE MASSEUSE.

VROOOM
THIS TIME LAVAL IS NOT SO LUCKY.
THIS BRIDGE IS MORE ELASTIC THAN I THOUGHT.
BOING
BOING

PHEW!
IT'S A TIE! SPARRATUS, GET THE SPIDER STALKER READY. MY CUCUMBER MASK HAS FINALLY DRIED.
I THOUGHT LIONS WERE ONLY AFRAID OF WATER.
AS YOU WISH, MY LADY. WHERE ARE WE GOING?
TO THE GORGE OF ETERNAL DEPTH.

IN THE MEANTIME, ERIS, CRAGGER, AND THE OTHER WARRIORS ARE PREPARING FOR THEIR FIRST NIGHT IN THE OPEN...
I CAN'T BELIEVE THAT LAVAL HAS LET US DOWN LIKE THIS.
MAYBE THERE'S ANOTHER REASON FOR IT...
CRACK
DID YOU HEAR THAT?
LET'S TAKE A LOOK.
WHERE ARE YOU BOUND FOR?
THE GORGE OF ETERNAL DEPTH. THE SPIDER QUEEN HAS CAPTURED THE LION WARRIOR AND THAT MASKED TROUBLEMAKER.
SHE IS MAKING THEM COMPETE AGAINST EACH OTHER.
OH, NO! LAVAL DIDN'T LEAVE US IN THE LURCH. HE'S BEEN KID-NAPPED!
IT'S NOT TOO LATE. YOU FLY TO THE GORGE. I'LL FETCH REINFORCE-MENTS.

FOR THE LAST CHALLENGE, SPINLYN HAS COME UP WITH SOMETHING REALLY SPECIAL...
THE ETERNAL DROP FROM THE CLIFF RAMP!
SHADOWIND IS THE FIRST TO HAZARD THE DEATH-DEFYING LEAP...
SEE YOU ON THE OTHER SIDE.
GOOD LUCK.
VRRROOOM
THAT WAS CLOSE. SHADOWIND WAS JUST A HAIR'S BREADTH FROM FALLING.
NOW IT'S LAVAL'S TURN. WILL HE SURVIVE THE LEAP FROM THE CLIFF RAMP OR WILL HE BE SWALLOWED BY THE ETERNAL DEPTH?

LAVAL HEADS TOWARDS THE RAMP...
RIGHT. LET'S DO IT!
...AND TAKES OFF.
VROOOOOMMMM
BUT IT'S NOT LOOKING GOOD FOR THE LION...
NOOOO!
WHAT?! WHAT'S GOING ON?
CRACK

ERIS HAS RESCUED HER FRIEND IN THE NICK OF TIME...
LAVAL, I'M SO SORRY. I THOUGHT YOU'D LEFT US ALONE BECAUSE OF THE SPEEDORZ TOURNAMENT. CAN YOU FORGIVE ME?
IT'S ALL RIGHT, ERIS. WITHOUT YOU I'D BE SPIDER FOOD BY NOW.
SPINLYN IS BESIDE HERSELF WITH RAGE.
YOU-- YOU CHEATED. THE LION WARRIOR CHEATED! SOLDIERS, SEIZE HIM!
TAKE YOUR HANDS OFF MY BEST BUDDY!
WE SHALL FINISH THIS ANOTHER TIME, CROCODILES. RIGHT NOW MY BEAUTY SLEEP IS MORE IMPORTANT.

WHO ARE YOU LOOKING FOR?
SHADOWIND. HE WAS STILL HERE A MOMENT AGO.
BUT SHADOWIND HAS ALREADY DISAPPEARED. WILL LAVAL EVER DISCOVER THE TRUE IDENTITY OF THE MYSTERIOUS RIDER?
THE END

In their search for the legend beasts, our heroes have found shelter in the shack of the hermit lion Lavertus. Here they can fortify themselves and hone their fighting skills...
UNDER THE SPELL OF THE SCORPIONS
This morning, Lavertus is giving the young warriors a lecture on the dangers of the Outlands...
...AND THE STRANGLER GRASS, WHICH DOESN'T LET GO OF ITS VICTIM UNTIL IT HAS GONE COMPLETELY STILL.
BUT MOST DANGEROUS OF ALL ARE THE SCORPIONS. WITH THE POISON IN THEIR TAILS THEY CAN GAIN CONTROL OVER ANY LIVING CREATURE. SO BEWARE OF THEIR STINGS!
LUCKILY WE'RE WELL PREPARED!
IS THERE AN ANTIDOTE OF SOME KIND?
THEY SAY THAT THE BLUE MOSS FROM THE SCORPION CAVE CAN CURE POISONING. BUT ONLY THE SCORPIONS KNOW WHERE THE CAVE IS.

AFTER THE LECTURE ABOUT THE TERRIBLE INHABITANTS OF THE OUTLANDS, LAVAL NEEDS TO DISTRACT HIMSELF FOR A WHILE...
HEY CRAGGER, UP FOR A SPEEDORZ RACE? I'M ALREADY STARTING TO FEEL RUSTY.
NOT UNTIL I'VE DESTROYED THIS PLANT HERE.
IT'S THE REASON WHY WE'VE FOUGHT AGAINST EACH OTHER SO OFTEN.
THE PLANT CAN'T HELP THAT. IT WAS JUST PUT TO THE WRONG USE.
WE MUST THINK OF A NAME FOR YOU, LITTLE FLOWER.
GORZAN! HE'S IN DANGER!
DON'T WORRY. THE PREDATOR PLANT IS NOWHERE BIG ENOUGH TO DEVOUR HIM.
NO, LOOK! THERE'S A MONSTER MOVING TOWARDS HIM!

THE LION WARRIOR DOESN'T HESITATE, LEAPING ONTO HIS SPEEDORZ.
GO AND WARN THE OTHERS. I'LL TRY TO HOLD IT BACK.
WOOOOOOW
I DON'T REMEMBER LAVERTUS SAYING ANYTHING ABOUT A VINE-MUD MONSTER.
OR MAYBE I WASN'T PAYING ATTENTION?
AT A LUCKY MOMENT, LAVAL MAKES A GRAB FOR A DANGLING VINE...
GOT IT!
VROOOOOM
...AND CIRCLES THE MONSTER'S LEGS. THE MONSTER TRIPS OVER ITS OWN FEET!

THE OTHER HEROES HURRY TO THE AID OF LAVAL AND GORZON...
SURRENDER, MONSTER! WE HAVE YOU SURROUNDED!
THAT'S NOT A MONSTER!
IT'S A GORILLA STRIKER!
G'LOONA!
G'LOONA HAS A WORRISOME MESSAGE FOR THE HEROES...
THE GORILLAS... THEY... THEY WANT TO ATTACK THE LION TEMPLE.
BUT THE GORILLA TRIBE IS THE MOST PEACE-LOVING IN ALL OF CHIMA!
NOT ANY MORE. THEY DESTROYED ALL OF THE FLOWERS.
A TRAMPLED FLOWER: THAT REALLY ISN'T LIKE THE GORILLAS AT ALL!
DON'T WORRY, YOUR FRIENDS WILL TAKE CARE OF IT. BUR FIRST YOU MUST GET SOME REST.

NOT LONG AFTERWARDS, LAVAL, CRAGGER, AND GORZAN ARE ON THEIR WAY TO CHIMA...
LET'S FIND OUT THE REASON FOR THE SUDDEN CHANGE OF HEART!
A WHILE LATER THEY REACH THE GORILLA FOREST...
BE AS QUIET AS POSSIBLE. WE GORILLAS CAN TURN PRETTY UN-GROOVY.
THE THREE FRIENDS CANNOT BELIEVE THEIR EYES...
GRIZZAM, HAVE YOU STILL GOT ROOM FOR A FEW FRIENDS OF OURS?
SURE, DUDE.
THE GORILLAS HAVE JOINED FORCES WITH THE SCORPIONS?!

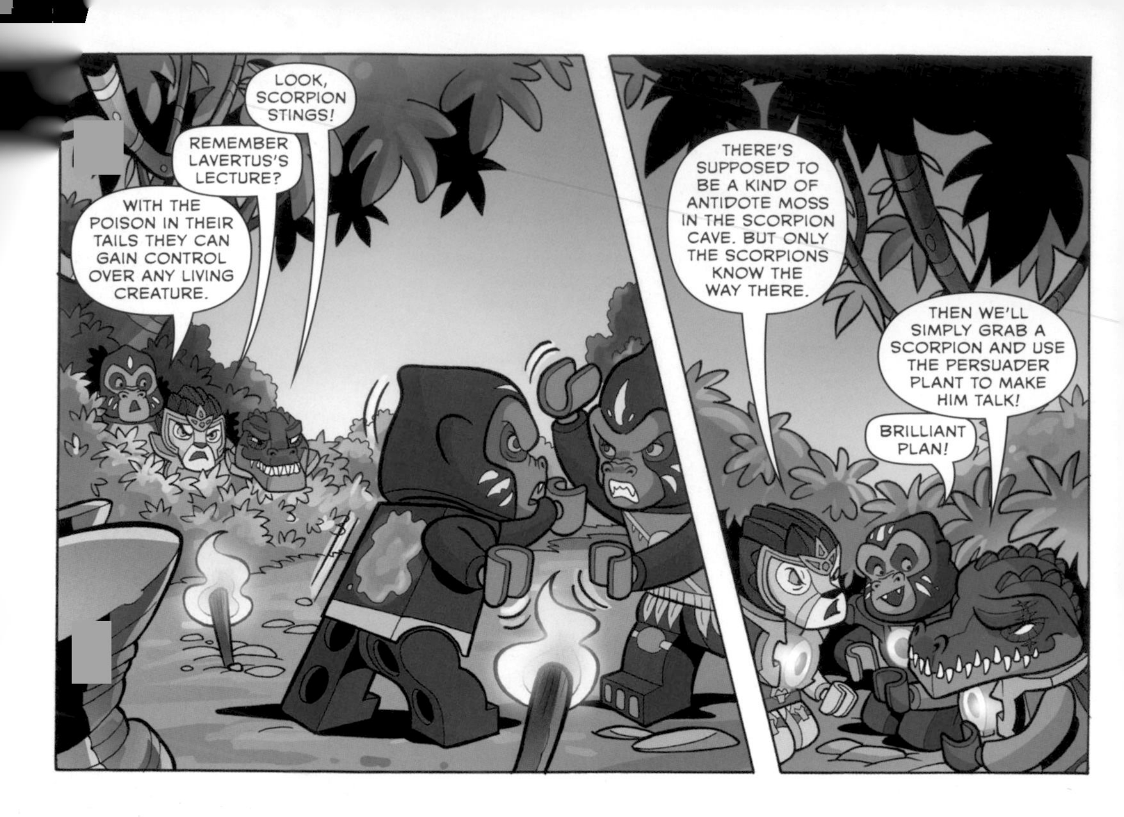
LOOK, SCORPION STINGS!
REMEMBER LAVERTUS'S LECTURE?
WITH THE POISON IN THEIR TAILS THEY CAN GAIN CONTROL OVER ANY LIVING CREATURE.
THERE'S SUPPOSED TO BE A KIND OF ANTIDOTE MOSS IN THE SCORPION CAVE. BUT ONLY THE SCORPIONS KNOW THE WAY THERE.
THEN WE'LL SIMPLY GRAB A SCORPION AND USE THE PERSUADER PLANT TO MAKE HIM TALK!
BRILLIANT PLAN!

SAID AND DONE...
THE SCORPION IS POWERLESS AGAINST THE FRAGRANCE OF THE MYSTERIOUS FLOWER.
TELL US THE WAY TO THE SCORPION CAVE!
FIRST YOU MUST GO TO THE ETERNAL GORGE. THERE, YOU TURN LEFT. AHEAD YOU WILL--

THANKS TO THE SCORPION'S PRECISE DIRECTIONS, THE THREE WARRIORS QUICKLY FIND THE TUNNEL LEADING TO THE SCORPION CAVE.
OVER THERE!

LAVAL, CRAGGER AND GORZON STAND WITH BATED BREATH. BEFORE THEM LIES THE REALM OF THE SCORPIONS, THE BREEDING GROUND OF ALL THAT IS EVIL.
WE CAN STILL GET AWAY.
NO. I MUST SAVE MY TRIBE.
IF WE DO NOTHING NOW, THE GORILLAS WILL ATTACK THE LIONS. WE CANNOT ALLOW THAT TO HAPPEN.
LAVAL MAKES AN INTERESTING DISCOVERY ON THE RIVERBANK.
THIS MOSS IS DIFFERENT FROM THE REST. IT MUST BE THE BLUE MOSS!
LAVAL? I THINK WE HAVE COMPANY...

IT LOOKS AS IF THE SCORPIONS SHARE THEIR HABITATION WITH ANOTHER TRIBE...
OH NO, BATS!
INTRUDERS!

TIME FOR SOME ACTION!

SCRAM, YOU MISERABLE FLAPPING VERMIN!
ARGH!
CRAGGER SUCCEEDS IN DRIVING OFF THE ATTACKERS WITH A BURST OF WARNING SHOTS.
POW

BUT NOW THE SCORPIONS HAVE NOTICED THE THREE UNINVITED GUESTS..
LET'S GRAB THE ANTIDOTE MOSS AND SOME CHI-- AND GET OUT OF HERE!
BUT HOW?
CRAGGER, YOU HAVE A VISITOR.

THE CROCODILE LEGEND BEAST!
YOU'VE COME JUST IN THE NICK OF TIME, BUDDY.
FOLLOW ME! WE'LL BE SAFE ON THE CROCODILE'S BACK!
THAT WAS REALLY CLOSE!

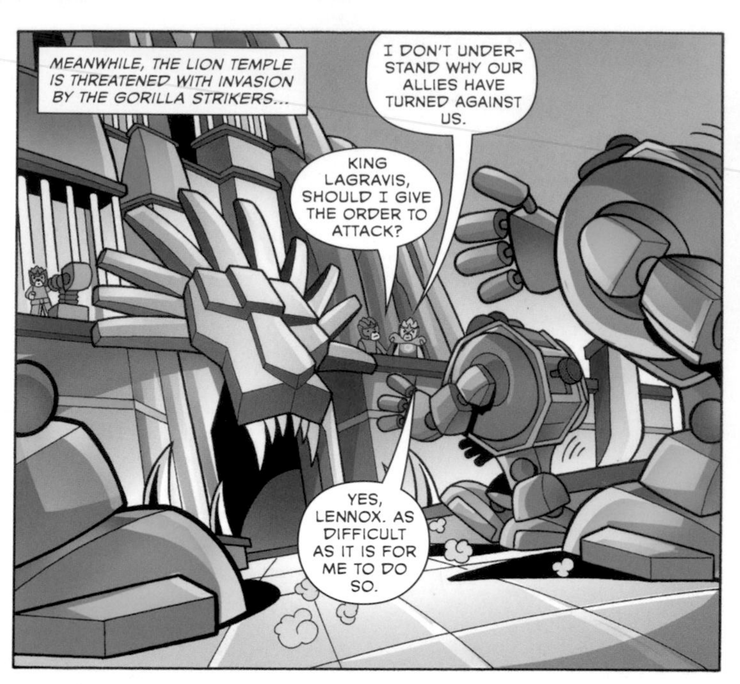
MEANWHILE, THE LION TEMPLE IS THREATENED WITH INVASION BY THE GORILLA STRIKERS...
I DON'T UNDERSTAND WHY OUR ALLIES HAVE TURNED AGAINST US.
KING LAGRAVIS, SHOULD I GIVE THE ORDER TO ATTACK?
YES, LENNOX. AS DIFFICULT AS IT IS FOR ME TO DO SO.

I DON'T BELIEVE MY EYES. IS THAT LAVAL STANDING DOWN THERE ON THE BRIDGE?!
STOP! HOLD YOUR FIRE!

ARE YOU READY?
READIER THAN READY!

ALL THREE USE A CHI ORB.
FOR CHIMA!

LAVAL STARTS BY TACKLING GRUMLO'S STRIKER...
GO AND FIND YOURSELF A LIFT SOMEWHERE ELSE!
HAVE A GOOD TRIP!
AAAAHHH!

EAT THIS, GORILLA!
THE GORILLA WASN'T EXPECTING THAT.
EVEN AS GRUMLO IS CHEWING, THE ANTIDOTE MOSS STARTS TO TAKE EFFECT. THE FIRST POISONING HAS BEEN CURED!
WHAT... WHAT HAPPENED?
THE SCORPIONS POISONED YOU AND HAVE TAKEN OVER THE OTHER GORILLAS' MINDS. BUT DON'T WORRY, WE'RE GOING TO RESCUE THEM AS WELL.

SOON AFTERWARDS, LAVAL, CRAGGER AND GORZON CURE THE GORILLAS...
WE OWE YOU A GREAT DEBT OF GRATITUDE. IF IT WEREN'T FOR YOU WE WOULD HAVE ATTACKED OUR FRIENDS.
DON'T MENTION IT. OH, THAT REMINDS ME...
WE HAVE A GIFT FOR YOU. SPECIAL ARMOR MADE BY OUR FRIEND LAVERTUS. TO PROTECT YOU FROM SCORPION STINGS IN THE FUTURE.
THE TIME IS APPROACHING TO RETURN TO THE OUTLANDS. AFTER ALL, THE HEROES ARE STILL FAR FROM HAVING FOUND ALL OF THE LEGEND BEASTS!
CRAGGER, SHALL WE GO?
RIGHT AWAY.
I'M SURE WE CAN PUT THE PLANT TO GOOD USE ANOTHER TIME.
MAYBE WE SHOULD USE IT ON RAZAR. THIS MORNING HE STOLE MY CUP-CAKES AGAIN...
IF YOU NEED ANY CARE TIPS, JUST ASK ME.
THE END

WATCH OUT FOR PAPERCUTZ

Welcome to the Chi-filled first LEGO® LEGENDS OF CHIMA graphic novel, by Yannick Grotholt and Comicon, from Papercutz, the animal-loving folks dedicated to publishing great graphic novels for all ages.

As I write these words, the recently released THE LEGO MOVIE is breaking all sorts of box office records as the #1 movie in North America. But even more exciting for us on a personal level, our LEGO NINJAGO #9 "Night of the Nindroids" is the #1 graphic book (paperback) on The New York Times best-seller list! And we can't think of any better way to celebrate LEGO's super-success than by publishing LEGO LEGENDS OF CHIMA—the graphic novel series you've been demanding to see!

Clearly, this is a great time to be a LEGO fan! But it keeps getting better! LEGO NINJAGO is back on Cartoon Network with several all-new specials, and LEGO LEGENDS OF CHIMA is also a huge hit on Cartoon Network! The excitement just doesn't seem to end!

And speaking of exciting, we've been meaning to mention for some time that our LEGO NINJAGO graphic novels are also published in Germany, as part of a LEGO NINJAGO magazine published by our friends at Blue Ocean. Now, our roles are reversed and we're publishing comics originally published first in the LEGO LEGENDS OF CHIMA comics magazine in Germany—translated into English, of course! So rather than getting one great big story like we usually present in LEGO NINJAGO, we're getting four stories from four issues of their magazine to publish in one of our graphic novels.

One of the interesting differences between a magazine and a graphic novel, is that Papercutz fans have come to expect complete stories in our books. The folks at Blue Ocean did something rather interesting with the ending of the "A Spark of Friendship" story—they added a cliff-hanger ending and asked LEGO fans to send in their ideas of how that story would end. We thought that might be a little bit confusing, so we brought in LEGO NINJAGO artist, Jolyon Yates, and colorist, Laurie E. Smith, to create a new last panel that more clearly concludes the story. But just for fun, here's a look at the original last two panels:

So, for the would-be-writers out there, here's your opportunity to tell us what you think happens next! Just send your ideas, scripts, etc., to the addresses listed below. We may showcase some of the best ones in a future LEGO LEGENDS OF CHIMA graphic novel.

In the meantime, keep an eye out for LEGO LEGENDS OF CHIMA #2 "The Right Decision" comic soon!

Long Live LEGO!

Thanks,

STAY IN TOUCH!

EMAIL: salicrup@papercutz.com
WEB: papercutz.com
TWITTER: @papercutzgn
FACEBOOK: PAPERCUTZGRAPHICNOVELS
FAN MAIL: Papercutz, 160 Broadway, Suite 700, East Wing, New York, NY 10038

LEGO® GRAPHIC NOVELS AVAILABLE FROM PAPERCUTZ™

LEGO NINJAGO #1

LEGO NINJAGO #2

LEGO NINJAGO #3

LEGO NINJAGO #4

LEGO NINJAGO #5

LEGO NINJAGO #6

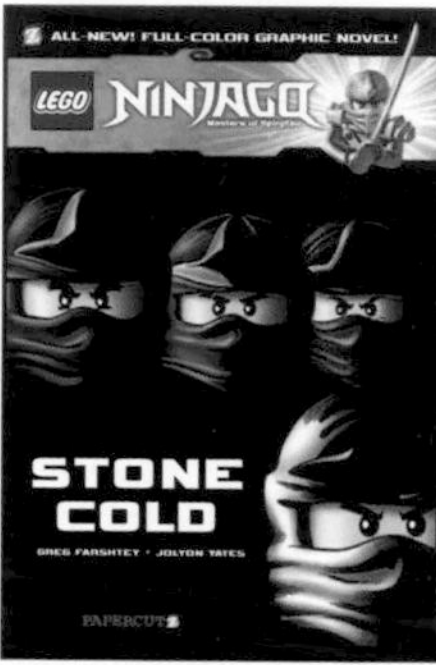

LEGO NINJAGO #7

LEGO NINJAGO #8

SPECIAL EDITION #1 (Features stories from NINJAGO #1 & #2.)

SPECIAL EDITION #2 (Features stories from NINJAGO #3 & #4.)

SPECIAL EDITION #3 (Features stories from NINJAGO #5 & #6.)

LEGO NINJAGO #9

LEGO® NINJAGO graphic novels are available in paperback and hardcover at booksellers everywhere.

LEGO® NINJAGO #1-10 are $6.99 in paperback, and $10.99 in hardcover. LEGO NINJAGO SPECIAL EDITION #1-3 are $10.99 in paperback only. You can also order online at papercutz.com. Or call 1-800-886-1223, Monday through Friday, 9 – 5 EST. MC, Visa, and AmEx accepted. To order by mail, please add $4.00 for postage and handling for first book ordered, $1.00 for each additional book and make check payable to NBM Publishing. Send to: Papercutz, 160 Broadway, Suite 700, East Wing, New York, NY 10038.

LEGO NINJAGO graphic novels are also available digitally wherever e-books are sold.

COMING SOON!

LEGO NINJAGO #10